P9-CLS-983

GOOD DEVILS